S. Strocel

Tampered

Michele Martin
Bossley

Orca currents

ORCA BOOK PUBLISHERS

Library and Archives Canada Cataloguing in Publication

Bossley, Michele Martin
Tampered / Michele Martin Bossley.
(Orca currents)

Issued also in electronic formats.
ISBN 978-1-4598-0357-2 (bound).--ISBN 978-1-4598-0356-5 (pbk.)

I. Title. II. Series: Orca currents
PS8553.O7394T36 2013   jc813'.54   C2013-901988-x

First published in the United States, 2013
Library of Congress Control Number: 2013935621

Summary: Three teenage amateur sleuths have to solve the mystery
of grocery-store food-tampering incidents.

*Orca Book Publishers is dedicated to preserving the environment and has
printed this book on Forest Stewardship Council® certified paper.*

Orca Book Publishers gratefully acknowledges the support for its
publishing programs provided by the following agencies: the Government
of Canada through the Canada Book Fund and the Canada Council for the Arts,
and the Province of British Columbia through the BC Arts Council
and the Book Publishing Tax Credit.

Cover photography by Getty Images

ORCA BOOK PUBLISHERS
PO Box 5626, Stn. B
Victoria, BC Canada
V8R 6S4

ORCA BOOK PUBLISHERS
PO Box 468
Custer, WA USA
98240-0468

www.orcabook.com
Printed and bound in Canada.

16 15 14 13 • 4 3 2 1

For Thyra,
Here's to childhood memories of games of
pretend, a shared love of books,
and wonderful imaginary adventures.
May the magic always be in us.

Chapter One

"So, Trevor, do you think you can handle it?"

"Absolutely," I said, pretending to be cool.

"Good." My new boss clapped me on the shoulder and handed me a broom. "We'll start you off easy. Someone spilled rice from the bulk bins.

Take care of that, and then we'll test you out bagging on register five."

"Okay," I said. "Sounds good." I wondered if I should call him Mr. O'Rourke, but that felt weird. Scott O'Rourke was around forty, but he treated me like an equal, even though I was fourteen and starting my first real job.

I took the broom and headed toward the bulk bins that lined the wall at the far end of the store. As I walked through the produce department, rice crunched under the slick soles of my new dress shoes.

"Whoa!" I hollered as I lurched and slid. I grabbed the closest object, a wooden bin stacked high with apples. I caught my balance, but not before sending the carefully built mountain of apples cascading to the floor. I grabbed as many as I could before they hit the ground, using my body, legs and green canvas apron to stop them from bruising. I had reached up to stop the flow of apples when two more pairs of hands joined mine, and the mini-avalanche stopped. I breathed a sigh of relief and looked at my rescuers. "Oh, it's you," I said in a sour voice. I felt my face turning red.

"Hi to you, too," Robyn said.

"Hey dude," my cousin Nick said. "Great start to your career."

I began putting the apples I'd managed to save back in the bin. "Yeah. I've only been on the job for ten minutes, and look what happens. I think that's a record. Why are you guys here, anyway?"

"We thought you might need some moral support on your first day," Robyn said, looking hurt.

"Besides, Alex wanted to come by," Nick said, gesturing to a short guy who was now picking up apples. He had black hair buzzed almost to the scalp, light brown skin dotted with pimples, and brown eyes that crinkled in the corners as he gave me a wide smile.

"Hey, Trev," he said, slapping my hand.

"Alex. It's been awhile, man," I said.

"Like, grade two. What's happening, dude?" Alex said.

"Not much. You?" Alex and I had started kindergarten together. He had been the kid with more energy than the entire class put together. He used to drive the teacher nuts. Then he moved somewhere up north, and we lost touch.

"Just moved back," Alex said. "My dad split, and my mom wanted to come home." He said this as if it didn't matter, but I saw a brief flash of pain in his eyes.

"Sorry to hear that, dude," I said.

"Yeah, well, whatever. I'm back. I thought I'd look up my old friends."

"Cool."

"I don't want to look up old friends. I want to laugh at your uniform," Nick said. "Nice shoes, dude." Nick looked over my shiny black dress shoes, black pants, white button-down shirt and green apron with *Ashton's Fresh Marketplace* printed in orange on the front.

"Urinate off, Nick, before you get me in trouble," I said, aware that staff were not supposed to swear at the customers even if one was related and 100 percent annoying.

Nick grinned. He seemed pleased that he had me in a position where I had to be polite and not put him in a choke hold. "No, I don't think so. I need to pick up some stuff for my mom. You have any idea where the stuffed olives are?"

"Olives? You hate olives."

"So, you know where they are?"

"Aisle four, I think. With the canned vegetables. You seriously want olives?"

"No, I was just testing you."

I clenched my hands into fists. Nick was a great friend and a good guy, but I didn't need this right now. He must have known that I was about to throttle him, job or no job, because he dropped his teasing grin.

"Sorry, dude. Just kidding. I have to get sandwich meat, milk and juice boxes though. And some grapes." Nick consulted a scrap of paper.

"Yeah," Alex chimed in. "We went by the vegetables, but there weren't any grapes."

I leaned the broom against the wall. "I can show you where that stuff is, but then you have to get out of here, okay?"

"No problem," Nick said. They followed me to the front of the produce aisle, where the grapes were displayed. I handed a bag to Nick.

"Those ones look better," Alex said, pointing to a bag higher up on the display.

I rolled my eyes. "They're all the same, Alex."

"Those ones are squished. If I were Nick, I wouldn't pay for squished grapes," said Alex.

I sighed and reached for the bag Alex wanted. As I lifted it, a small black spider fell out, skittered across my wrist and landed somewhere in the rest of the grapes. I yelped.

"Holy crap, that's a black widow!"

Nick and Robyn looked at me in horror, but Alex was fighting to keep his expression neutral. He snorted a few times, and when I gave him my best penetrating stare, he broke into helpless laughter.

"You noob!" I said in disgust. "It was fake, wasn't it?"

Alex nodded, unable to speak. Finally, he said, "You should have seen your face, man. I knew Nick was getting grapes, so I couldn't resist."

"Alex, grow up!" Robyn shook her head.

"You guys better go—" I broke off as an angry voice interrupted us.

"This is completely unfair, Scott, and you know it!" a woman nearly shouted from the next aisle.

"Shhhh!" I heard someone else say.

"Don't you shush me!" The woman's voice was laced with venom. "How can you justify taking away my shifts? I've worked here for five years. I've got two kids to support, you know."

"Look, Mattie. Let's go into my office and discuss it—"

"I don't think so," Mattie shot back. "We'll discuss it right now!"

Alex, Robyn, Nick and I exchanged glances. At the end of the aisle, we peered around a display of soup cans to see my boss facing a thirty-something woman with flyaway brown hair. It stood out in wispy strands like a wild halo around her face, and her gaze was fixed in mean dislike on my boss. She reminded me of a Pomeranian dog I used to see on my newspaper route—yappy and aggressive, with a similar ruff of wild brown hair.

"Who's that?" Robyn whispered to me.

I shrugged. "Employee, I guess," I whispered back.

Scott's back was to us. I saw him raise his hand in a placating gesture. "Mattie, believe me, it wasn't an easy decision…"

"Oh, it was easy, all right," retorted Mattie. "You just took a pen and crossed me off the list."

Scott straightened. "You have repeatedly not shown up for your assigned shifts, and you're often late, sometimes by more than thirty minutes. I have junior staff who show up on time and make a point of being here as scheduled."

"Your junior staff don't have to wait for a babysitter," Mattie argued, her mouth twisting as if she had swallowed something bitter. "They just have mommy or daddy drive them to part-time jobs, so they can buy new snowboards or computer games."

Scott sighed. "Mattie, I understand your difficulties, but how my staff spend their money isn't my concern. My concern is running this store, and I need reliable workers. Bottom line."

"You got an answer for everything, but no one can trust a word you say!" Mattie retorted. "You told me it wasn't a problem, that you'd be flexible."

"I can't be flexible with a no-show employee. You have to be here on schedule."

"It isn't that easy, you donkey's backside!" Mattie yelled. "I can't leave my kids at home alone!"

"I'm sorry, Mattie," Scott said, his anger obvious in spite of his tight control. "But I won't stand for disrespect, and you've already proven I can't trust you to do your job."

"So what are you saying?" Mattie's face suddenly paled.

"I'm saying—" Scott drew himself up to his full height. "That you're fired."

Chapter Two

I held my breath. Robyn and Nick crowded behind me, trying to see around the soup cans. Alex knelt on the floor and peered around the bottom of the flat.

"You can't fire me, you lousy bag of crap. I QUIT!" Mattie shrieked the last word, pushed past Scott and headed my way. She bashed into me, knocking me into the display, and soup cans flew. Alex ducked.

As Nick pulled me up, Mattie fixed her bulging eyes on me. She was breathing heavily as she shook her finger in my face. "You listen to me, kid. You think you've got a sweet job, but you just wait. First chance they get, they'll treat you like dirt. A pile of—"

Scott reached for Mattie's elbow. "You'd better leave."

Mattie shook him off. "Don't touch me!" she spat. "I'm going." She spun away and barreled down the aisle to the store's front door. Within seconds, she was gone.

Robyn drew a shaky breath. No one knew what to say.

I began picking up the fallen soup cans, but Scott stopped me.

"Never mind that right now, Trevor," he said. "I'm really sorry you had to witness that. Mattie was an efficient employee. I'm sorry to see her go."

"It's fine," I mumbled.

"No, it isn't fine," Scott said. "It's your first day. I don't want you thinking I'm some kind of an ogre. I told Mattie the truth—she's missed way more than a few shifts and left us short-staffed, which isn't fair to anyone. If she'd been responsible about calling in replacements, or even letting me know she couldn't make it, I wouldn't have cut back her hours. But Ashton's is a good store, and our customers depend on our employees. I don't like upsetting people, but I have to run the store properly. It's my job."

"I understand," I said.

"Take a second before you head back to work," Scott said.

Alex, Nick and Robyn stared at me. "That was quite a scene," Robyn said at last.

"Tell me about it," I said. "That woman looked angry enough to shoot someone."

"Be glad she didn't," Nick said, unusually serious. "Sometimes people in her situation lose it and do something stupid."

"I think we should go," Robyn said.

"Scared?" Nick asked.

"No. But I think that Trevor has had enough trouble for one afternoon, and we're not helping. Maybe you should ask if you can go home, Trevor."

"On my first day?" I said. "That's a good way to lose my job. I haven't done anything yet except knock over a bunch of apples and a stack of cans."

"You could claim you're traumatized by the incident," Robyn said.

"And look like a wimp. Good idea, Robyn," Nick said.

I was starting to say I was fine when a terrified scream echoed through the store.

Adrenalin shot through me like an electric jolt. Had Mattie come back for revenge?

Fighting the urge to run for the nearest exit, the four of us backtracked toward the produce department, where the screaming continued. Mattie was nowhere to be seen. An elderly lady raised a mammoth purse over her head and swung it down with terrific force into the display of grapes. Purple juice spattered her glasses, and grapes rained onto the floor. She lifted the purse again.

"Ma'am, wait!" I called, racing over. "What are you doing?"

"Spider. Black widow," she puffed, slamming her purse into the grapes a second time. "Gave me a nasty shock to see the critter, but I'll get 'im."

"No, wait. I'll do it," I said, shooting Alex an accusing glance. "I wouldn't want you to get hurt."

"What's going on?" Scott had rushed up.

The old lady turned on him. "Are you the manager?"

"I am."

"Then you should know that you have black widows in your grapes. A fancy store like yours should do a better job checking the produce."

"A black widow? Really?" Scott stared at the squished grapes. "Was it alive?"

"I didn't stop to ask it," the lady retorted.

Scott picked through the ruined bags of grapes.

"I'd wear gloves if I were you," the old lady advised. By now a crowd had gathered. Scott wrapped his hands in plastic produce bags and used a cucumber as a makeshift stick. He rummaged through the grapes, eventually pulling out a black wiggly thing. "It's rubber," Scott said with disgust. He eyed my friends suspiciously, and Alex turned red. "Some kid must have left it here."

"Rubber!" the old lady fumed. "You mean we went through all this for a fake spider? If Ashton's can't keep people from meddling with their products, then I'm shopping somewhere else. My heart can't take this!" She plucked up her purple-stained purse and marched out the door.

The crowd began to melt away, and I turned to Alex, half expecting him to confess, but only Nick and Robyn remained. Alex had disappeared.

Chapter Three

"Alex, that was soy sauce, not vanilla!" I clutched my hair with both hands. "The entire batch is ruined!"

"Heh-heh-heh." Alex couldn't hide a snicker.

I rounded on him. "Did you do that on purpose?" I said, furious. "You idiot! You already messed me up with that stupid spider trick at work."

"It was a just a joke, Trevor. Chill, dude."

"I can't chill. If my boss knew one of my friends planted that spider, I'd get fired."

"But no one got hurt," Alex said.

"That's not the point," I said. "And now you've wrecked this project. I can't fail Foods class. My math marks are horrible. I need my grade in this class to bring my average up, not down."

Alex looked contrite. "Sorry, dude. I guess we'll have to start over." Alex sighed.

"We can't. We've used all our bananas," I said.

Alex considered the situation. "Just bake it anyway," he said. "It'll still look okay. As long as Ms. T doesn't taste it, she won't flunk us," Alex said.

I frowned. "She has to taste it to give us a mark."

"I'll think of something," Alex promised. He stirred the batter, scraped it into the loaf pan and pushed it into the oven, sticking the thumb of the oven mitt into the batter in the process. "Argh." He shut the oven door and tried to scrape the goo off the mitt with a spoon. "Why does cooking look so easy on TV?"

"Cut it out. You're getting batter on the floor," I said.

"How's it going there, boys?" Ms. Thompson asked from behind us. She eyed the mess. "Too bad I don't offer laundry classes, Alex."

"I can wash it," Alex said. "Just tell me what to do."

"No. No, that's okay," Ms. Thompson said hastily. "I don't have any money in the budget to replace oven mitts. You guys start cleaning up. The banana loaf needs to bake for about forty minutes, so we should be able to put it to a taste test just before the bell." She moved off to inspect the next group's work, and Alex and I looked at each other in alarm.

"Now what?" I said.

"I don't know!" Alex answered.

"You said you'd figure it out," I said through gritted teeth.

"Okay, I'm on it. Let me think." Alex began putting away ingredients.

I filled the sink with hot water and soap and started washing the dishes. We worked in silence until the oven timer in the next workstation went off.

I watched as Lauren pulled a loaf out of her oven. It smelled fantastic. Ours... not so much. I peeked through the oven window. It was lopsided and giving off an odor like chow mein.

"What stinks?" Alex asked.

"Our banana bread," I answered.

Alex frowned. "This could be bad for us," he said.

"Tell me something I don't know," I snapped.

Alex glanced around the class. Ms. T was at the far side of the room.

"Psst. Lauren!" Alex hissed. She looked up from the bread she was cutting into neat slices. The scent made my mouth water, which was a whole lot nicer than the gag reflex that kicked in when Alex yanked our soggy, smelly bread out of the oven. "Give me a couple pieces of your banana bread."

Lauren stared down her nose at him. "No."

"Aww, come on, Lauren. Give a dude a break. Trevor is going to fry my butt if he flunks this class. Look at this mess we cooked." He held up our loaf pan.

"It doesn't look so bad, but it smells horrible," Lauren said.

"Exactly. Ms. Thompson is not going to be thrilled with this. Please, Lauren?"

Alex said. "Just give us one piece, so Ms. Thompson doesn't have us arrested for trying to poison her."

Lauren looked at me. I shrugged and gave her a sheepish grin.

"Oh, all right." Lauren's cheeks were pink as she handed over a slice of her loaf.

"Excellent! Thank you." Alex cut several slices of our banana bread, laid Lauren's piece carefully on top and hid the rest of the loaf under a dish-towel. He rubbed his hands together in glee. "We're saved, Trev. We give Ms. Thompson the bogus piece, she thinks we're geniuses, and you make the honor roll. All thanks to Lauren." He elbowed me in the ribs. "She likes you, man. That's why she handed over the goods."

I was opening my mouth to tell Alex that this was never going to work when Ms. Thompson came by to check our progress.

"All done, guys?" she asked.

"Yup," Alex said. "Want to sample a piece?" He held the plate out with a flourish.

Ms. Thompson took the top slice, just as planned. "Something smells a bit funny," she said.

"We...uh...experimented a little. But taste how good it is," Alex said.

Ms. Thompson bit into it. "Mmmm. Delicious. Whatever you boys did, it was the right thing." She popped the rest of the piece into her mouth.

Alex beamed.

"I need each of you to taste it as well. You're self-grading on this project," Ms. Thompson said.

"Self-grading?" Alex's expression faded.

"Yes. You and Trevor need to give each other a grade, based on your results, effort in the kitchen and cleanup. Not that you need to worry about the results.

They're fabulous!" said Ms. Thompson. "Go on." She nodded toward the plate.

Alex and I exchanged desperate glances. He looked like a prisoner about to be led to the guillotine. Knowing there was no other choice, I took a piece of our loaf. So did Alex.

I felt my lips curl as I brought the slice to my lips. I held my breath and bit into it, but the taste of squishy bananas with soy sauce was awful. I choked and spat the bite into my hand at the same moment Alex coughed, spitting his all over the floor.

"Eeew! Gross!" Lauren squealed from the next workstation.

"It's all right. I'm okay!" Alex stood up. "I just feel a little queasy. Must be a stomach flu."

Ms. Thompson eyed him with suspicion. "You seemed okay a minute ago."

"Very sudden, some of these flu bugs." Alex wiped his mouth with the back of his hand.

"At the exact moment Trevor gagged as well?" Ms. Thompson cocked an eyebrow at him. "I think it has more to do with this banana bread. Go rinse your mouth, Alex." She picked up a second piece and sniffed it. "It definitely smells different than the first piece." She nibbled at a corner, and she grimaced. "This is terrible," she said as Alex rejoined us. "What's the story here?"

"Uh…" I looked at Alex. "Alex used soy sauce instead of vanilla. All the bananas were gone, so we couldn't start over, and we baked it anyway."

"And the first piece I tasted?" Ms. Thompson said.

I avoided making eye contact with her. "We talked Lauren into giving us a piece of hers so we wouldn't fail the project."

"Well, that plan didn't work, did it?" Ms. Thompson snapped. "Didn't it occur to you that you were cheating?"

Alex looked at her in alarm. "No, not really. I mean, I knew it was wrong, but I didn't think of it as cheating. It's banana bread, not math."

"Well, it is cheating. Passing off another student's work as your own is cheating, whether it's math or science or cooking."

"What are you going to do?" I asked anxiously.

Ms. Thompson's glare could have melted iron. "I'm going to flunk you on this project and send a note home to your parents. Foods class should have a little more importance. Cooking is a life skill. When you're grown up and living on your own, you can't eat a math test. And switching ingredients is not only a bad idea when you're trying to make something taste good, it can be dangerous, too. Take this banana bread. I'm allergic to soy. What if I'd actually eaten it?"

I gulped. "That would have been bad."

"Yes. Lucky for you, I don't get a severe reaction, but some people do."

"We're really sorry." I sighed. "We didn't mean to cheat. And neither of us thought about it being dangerous."

"I understand, but next time, talk to me about it," Ms. Thompson said. "Maybe you can make the project up in another class, or during lunch hour."

"Okay," we both said.

She gestured to the mess on the floor. "I'll alert your teachers in your next classes that you'll be late. Go get a mop!"

Chapter Four

"Thanks, Trevor," Madison said with a smile as I finished bagging a massive cartload of groceries for a mom with three little kids. "It's been so busy tonight. You haven't even had time for a break yet. Why don't you go now? It's slowed down a little. I can handle it."

"That'd be great. I'm starving," I said. The store had been crowded all evening, mostly with after-work shoppers, but everyone seemed to be getting big orders. I'd bagged groceries as fast as I could all night. Alex and Nick had stopped in, but I hadn't been able to talk to them.

The store closed in an hour, so I decided to grab a quick snack. I wandered through the store, rejecting the carob energy bars, the carrot-granola crunchies and the dried-mango trail mix.

The bakery department's bulk bins were almost empty, but I scooped a handful of ginger cookies from one bin into a bag. Madison rang them through for me at the cash. Too hungry to wait until I got to the staff room, I opened the bag and stuffed a whole cookie into my mouth. I chewed rapidly, gulped it down and reached for another. It was on the second bite that my tongue began to burn. Then my whole throat felt like it had been engulfed in fire. I coughed. My eyes watered and then began to stream.

I coughed harder, spraying cookie crumbs on the floor.

"Trevor?" I felt Madison touch my shoulder. By now I could hardly see. "Are you okay?"

I shook my head. "Hot!" I sputtered. "Water!"

Madison left and returned within seconds. She held a water bottle to my lips. "Drink," she commanded.

I obeyed, letting the cool water flow over my burning tongue and throat. I gulped and gulped. Slowly the pain began to subside, but the tingling heat remained, and I could not swallow it away.

"Better?" Madison asked.

I nodded. "What's with those cookies?" I said, my voice hoarse.

"What do you mean?" said Madison.

I held up the bag. "I was fine until I ate these."

Madison grabbed the bag from me and sniffed it. "We'd better tell Scott.

There's something wrong here." She ran off toward customer service. I waited as an old gentleman walked up to the register.

"You open?" he said.

I shook my head. "Sorry. I'm new, but the clerk will be back soon."

"You okay, boy? You sound like you swallowed a truckload of gravel," he said.

I laughed, pain stabbing my throat. "I feel like it, too. I ate something that burned my throat."

The man looked at me sharply. "What sort of something?"

Before I could answer, Scott and Madison hurried up. "Trevor, what happened? Are you okay?" Scott said. I nodded, but before I could explain, the old man interrupted me.

"What did you eat?" he demanded.

Madison showed him the cookies.

"I'm a retired paramedic," he explained. "Can you breathe okay?"

he asked me. "Any feeling of swelling in your throat?"

"No," I croaked. The man checked the skin on the insides of my arms, my neck and face.

"No sign of hives or any reaction. You allergic to anything?" he said.

"No," I croaked again.

"Let's have a look at those cookies," said the old man. He dumped them onto the checkout counter, and both he and Scott peered at them. The old man picked one up, felt around the edges, broke it open and checked inside. Nothing looked unusual. Then he sniffed it and immediately sneezed. He ran one finger along the cinnamon-dusted top and touched it to his tongue.

"Ack!" He coughed. "There's your answer," he sputtered, looking at Scott and me. "These cookies are coated with cayenne pepper."

Chapter Five

"Cayenne pepper?" I said. "What's that?"

"Powdered red chili peppers. Extremely hot. Not something you'd expect to be in cookies." The old man directed a piercing stare in Scott's direction.

Scott's face turned red. "Obviously," he said coldly. "Someone in the bakery must have used the wrong ingredients by mistake."

"Maybe…although I've never heard of any baked goods that use cayenne," the man said. "But you'd better call the police as well as your bakery staff."

"The police?" Scott froze. "Why?"

"Because," the old man snapped, "you have no way of knowing how many people bought cookies that are full of pepper from that bakery today. You need to get the word out, and that means the police need to know. And if someone put cayenne in those cookies on purpose, that's a criminal investigation."

"That's going to mean press releases and the media, too." Scott blanched.

The old man nodded. "Yes."

"That could ruin the store."

"Probably not, but you'll have some negative publicity for a while," the old man said. Seeing Scott's hesitation, he lost patience. "Look, you've got no choice. If you withhold this information, you'll be held responsible if anyone gets hurt."

"But cayenne pepper isn't dangerous," Scott said.

"Do you really want to take that chance? What if someone eats one of those cookies while driving a car? Look at the kid's reaction. Is it worth the risk?"

Scott sighed. "No, no it's not. I'll call right away."

"Good." The old man gave me a pat on the shoulder. "Glad you're okay, kid. I'd like to be on my way, but if you need me as a witness, you can give me a call. I'll leave you my number."

"Thanks," Scott said. He fumbled for a pen and searched for something to write on, finally pulling a folded-up paper from his pocket. The old man scribbled his name and number on the top and bottom, tearing the paper in two. He handed one half to me, the other to Scott.

"Just in case you or the police have any questions. Good luck, kid. Your tongue should be back to normal in a day or so." He grinned at me. "Next time, try an apple. Healthier, and no surprises!"

Chapter Six

"All right, Alex. Let's get this right this time. I can't afford any more bad marks." I cracked an egg into the bowl.

"No problem," Alex said confidently. "Schnitzel is easy. I watched my grandpa make it all the time."

"Schnitzel? I thought we were making fried chicken," I said.

"Everyone else is making fried chicken. *We*," Alex paused dramatically, "are making schnitzel."

"Let's just follow the recipe, okay?" I said.

"Trevor, we need something awesome, something amazing, to pull our mark up after the banana-bread disaster. Schnitzel *is* fried chicken, only better."

"I thought schnitzel was made with veal or something," I said.

"Not if you make it with chicken," Alex pointed out.

"Okay, but Alex, I seriously don't want to fail this course. If you think you can pull this off, great. But if you can't, I'm dead. My average will hit bottom. My parents will kill me."

"You worry too much, Trevor." Alex pulled a package of chicken breasts out of the refrigerator and began rummaging in the utensil drawer. He came up with a wooden mallet.

"What's that for?" I asked.

"We have to pound the chicken breasts flat, then dip them in eggs and roll them in cracker crumbs and spices. Then we fry them. See? Fried chicken?"

"No one else is doing that."

"Ms. Thompson will love it." Alex put the chicken on the counter and wound up with the mallet. He slammed it down on the chicken, which shot out from under the mallet and slithered to the floor before either of us could catch it. "Great." Alex bent to pick it up with two fingers, gingerly surveying the chicken.

"Better wash it," I said.

"You do it." He tossed the chicken to me like it was a slimy softball. "I'll work on the other pieces."

I surveyed the chicken in my hands with distaste. I didn't feel even remotely like eating it. Stepping up to the sink, I rinsed the chicken first in cold water, then in hot. Most of the fuzz washed right off, but there were still some specks left, so I grabbed the dish soap and poured some on. I worked up a good lather. The specks floated off in the foam, and I gave the chicken a quick rinse. "Okay, it's ready," I said.

Alex had already prepared the other chicken pieces and was dropping them into a frying pan filled with about an inch of smoking oil. The oil spat and popped. "Ow!" he yelped. "Fix that piece yourself, Trevor. I'm kind of busy here."

"What do I do first?" I asked.

"Hit it with that wooden hammer." Alex kept his eyes on the frying pan.

I laid the piece of chicken on the counter and kept one hand on it while I whacked it with the mallet a few times. I held it up. The edges were bedraggled and a few bits were dangling, but I decided it would do. "Now what?"

Alex frowned in frustration. "Do I have to tell you everything? Dip it in the eggs and cover it in the bread crumbs, then put it in here."

"Okay, okay." I swished the chicken in what was left of the eggs Alex had beaten and dropped it onto the plate of bread crumbs. I flipped it over to make sure the crumbs coated the whole thing. I added my piece of chicken to the others in Alex's pan. It made a loud sizzle, and hot oil spattered all over the stove. Alex and I stepped back so we wouldn't get hit.

"Class, when your chicken is finished cooking, please bring it to your table so I can mark your effort, and then we can sample it," Ms. Thompson called from another kitchen station. "I bought some fresh buns from Ashton's Market, so we can make chicken sandwiches. Hope you remembered not to bring lunch today, unless you're really hungry!"

My eyes widened. *Ashton's Market.* I put up my hand but didn't wait for her to see me. "Ms. T!" I yelled across the room. "We can't use those buns. Didn't you see the news? Someone tampered with bakery cookies from Ashton's. The police are telling everyone to throw out anything they bought from the bakery or bring it back to the store."

Ms. Thompson stepped over to us. "Trevor, are you sure? I never watched the news last night, but—"

"I'm sure," I interrupted. "I work there, Ms. T. The whole bakery has been shut down for a couple of days while they investigate. Someone put cayenne pepper in the cookies, but the police don't know if that's the only thing that's been messed with or not."

"Well, thanks for letting me know," Ms. Thompson said. "I'll toss those buns in the trash right away."

"Wait!" I said. "We should check to see if there are any signs they've been tampered with. The police would want to know if there are more incidents."

Ms. Thompson looked impressed. "Good thinking, Trevor. I'll take a look." She walked to her desk, where several Ashton's bags sat.

Alex was shaking his head. "Throwing out everything from the store bakery is dumb."

"Yeah," I said. "The store is full of surveillance cameras. How could someone walk around sprinkling things with cayenne pepper and not get caught?"

"Have you ever seen people shop?" said Alex. "Old guys are always squeezing the buns to see if they're fresh. All they'd have to do is pretend to check the cookies and they could do almost anything. The cameras didn't catch me putting a rubber spider in the grapes."

I thought about that. If Alex was right, then the obvious suspect was Mattie, the woman who had been fired. She definitely had a reason to be angry at the store.

I turned to tell Alex, but my eye was drawn past him. I gave an unmanly squeak of horror. "Alex! The chicken is on fire!"

Alex spun around. "Holy crap! Trevor, get the fire extinguisher!"

I looked frantically for it. Flames shot up from the pan, and oily black smoke billowed around the hood fan. "Turn on the fan," I shouted. "The smoke alarms are going to go off!" I spotted a fire extinguisher strapped to a cabinet. I wrenched it down and fumbled with the pin to release the mechanism.

"Hurry up!" Alex yelled, his voice frantic.

"Wait, Trevor," Ms. Thompson said in a calm voice. "It's all right." She moved quickly, clapping a lid over the pan. Using an oven mitt, she removed the pan from the burner and turned off the heat. Smoke leaked in wisps from the edges of the lid for a few seconds, then stopped. Ms. Thompson lifted the lid to reveal several pieces of charred chicken.

"Doing some Cajun cooking, boys?" she asked.

"Huh?" Alex said.

"You know—blackened?" Ms. Thompson joked. "You had the heat up too high. Oil should never smoke."

"I didn't know," Alex said as he stared at the wreck of our chicken.

"This piece isn't too bad," Ms. Thompson said, pointing to one that wasn't quite as black as the others. She pulled it out with a fork and slid it onto a plate.

I recognized that piece. "That's—" I began.

"It might taste a little smoky, but I can still mark you guys on this," Ms. Thompson said.

"But that's the one I—" I broke off as Ms. Thompson cut a bite from the chicken and popped it into her mouth. A puzzled expression passed over her face as she chewed.

"There's a very unusual flavour here," she said. "It tastes like…" She grimaced. "Dish soap."

Alex rounded on me. "Didn't you wash the soap off?"

"Yeah, of course I did!" I said.

Ms. Thompson closed her eyes in great weariness. "Why did I choose teaching? Why didn't I go in for something easier—like nuclear physics or logging?" She opened her eyes. "Do you boys want to explain why you marinated your chicken in dish soap?"

Alex and I looked at each other. "You first," he said.

Chapter Seven

"Trevor, could you cover for me?" Madison said, untying her Ashton's apron and wadding it up under the customer-service desk. "I'm supposed to go on my break."

I looked up from the bin of returned goods. "Uh, sure. But I haven't been trained on customer service yet."

"It's no big deal. It's slow tonight anyway, and Brenda will be back from her break any minute. Please, Trevor?"

"Well, okay," I said. In the last week, there had been six more tampering incidents. More bakery items had been coated with cayenne. The bulk bins had also been targeted. Powdered lemonade had been poured into the oatmeal, and sugar had been dumped into a bin of soup mix. They were the kinds of things a kid might do, and I had a hard time pushing the thought of Alex's love of pranks out of my mind. As word got out, the decrease in customers was drastic. I'd gone from being so busy I had no time for a break to having almost nothing to do.

"Thanks!" Madison shot me a smile and trotted off to the magazine display. I dropped some organic shampoo from the return bin into a shopping cart, along with some sealed packages of candy, bottles of herbal remedies and a box of cereal. One of my jobs was to put returned items that were still saleable back on the shelves.

"Hey, kid. How's the tongue?"

I glanced over my shoulder and saw the retired paramedic who had helped me when I ate the cayenne pepper cookies. I grinned. "Cooled off a bit now," I said.

"Good. Got another problem for you." He dumped an Ashton's bag on the counter and removed a silver-foil bag of coffee. He jerked open the resealable closure, and we both stared at the ground coffee.

"What's wrong with it?" I said at last.

"Smell it," he said.

I took a whiff. "Yuck. That doesn't smell like any coffee I've ever known."

"That's because it's full of powdered garlic," the old guy said.

"Is that some new flavor or something?" I asked, puzzled.

"No, kid. It's because somebody put it there. I thought it smelled weird when it was brewing. I tasted the darn stuff to be sure. Garlic gives me terrible gas. I burped all morning from that one sip. I had a look at the bag. It had been glued shut. Someone's opened it, filled it up with garlic and resealed it."

"Gross! Why would anyone do that?" I said.

"Why would anyone try to burn your tongue off with pepper cookies?" the old guy countered. I didn't know what to say to that.

"You'd better get your manager, kid. Tampering with food is something the police need to know about."

"Right. Uh, I think he's in his office."

"I'll come with you." He picked up the bag of coffee and followed me to the back of the store. I led him through the double door to the stock area and loading dock, and we threaded our way through flats and boxes of various foods and up the stairs to Scott's office. I knocked on the half-open door and stuck my head into the cramped, windowless office. Scott paused in the middle of squirting hot sauce all over his deli sandwich, which was spread out on its wrapping over piles and piles of paperwork.

"Trevor!" he snapped, glancing from me to the old guy. "Customers aren't allowed up here. Why didn't you have me paged?"

The old guy rescued me. "Because he didn't think you wanted everyone in the store to know there's been another tampering incident until you've had a chance to inform police."

Scott's eyes widened. "What do you mean, another tampering incident?"

The old guy showed him the bag of coffee. "Mixed with garlic. Glue on the bag. You can see where someone has opened it very carefully and then glued it shut again."

"You're sure?" Scott said.

"Can't mistake garlic in your morning coffee, can you? It's not a common ingredient," the old guy retorted. "The police need to know. You might have to shut down the store for a few days to search this place."

Scott gripped the hot-sauce bottle like it was a lifeline, his knuckles white. "I can't do that!"

"You have no choice!" the old guy barked. "Any item in the store could be affected."

"It's probably just a kid," Scott argued. "I'm pretty sure one of Trevor's friends put a rubber spider in the grapes a few weeks ago." Scott glared at me. "We've had a few more minor things like that happen recently. It's probably just another random prank."

"It's not random. You had cookies that nearly burnt off the kid's tongue less than a week ago. And this doesn't look like the work of a kid to me," the old guy said. "Whoever opened this was careful to make sure that nothing looked out of the ordinary, otherwise I'd never have bought it. Someone spent time doing this. A kid would never do that. I think someone bought this item, fiddled with it at home and returned it to the store. What's your policy on returns?"

"Anything that is factory-sealed and in saleable condition can go back on the shelf. We don't put anything back that is packaged in the store, like meats or baked goods. Perishable items like produce don't go back," Scott said.

"So someone took the trouble to make this look like this coffee was still factory-sealed," the old guy said. "I'd start going through all your return slips for the past month or so."

Scott groaned. "That job alone could take months! They don't pay me enough to deal with this garbage." He stood up, shoved the bottle of hot sauce into a Ziploc bag and threw it in a desk drawer. "I'm obviously not going to get any lunch today," he said, crumpling the wrapper around the sandwich and pitching it into a garbage can. It hit the bottom with a hollow thud. "And even if I did go through all the return slips, if it was a straight exchange, if the customer told us they made a mistake and needed decaf or something, we would just have exchanged the item and marked it on their receipt. We don't even have a paper trail for that."

"Look, just call the police and quit whining. You're a lot more concerned about how much work this is going to cause you than you are about public safety," the old guy said.

Scott frowned. "There's been no threat to public safety."

"So far," the old guy said. "But who knows what's next? You can't let this go on. And your job is to maintain this store."

"I don't need you to tell me my job," Scott said, his eyes narrowing.

"I think you do." The old guy stood his ground.

"Uh, I'll start checking the other bags of coffee," I said, trying to break the tension. I felt invisible.

Scott finally glanced at me. "Good idea. You can show this gentleman out. I'll call the cops."

"Good," the old guy said, his voice filled with quiet threat. "Make sure you do." We left the office, and I walked through the store with the old guy. As we neared the doors, he turned to me. "I think your boss is more worried about the bad publicity from a police investigation. I don't trust him. You still have my number?"

I nodded. "I think it's in my other pants."

"Good. Call me if your boss doesn't take this seriously. I'll talk to the police myself."

"Okay."

"See you around, kid." He walked out of the store.

Chapter Eight

"Okay, Alex. This is it," I said in my most threatening tone. "We are going to follow the recipe today, even if it kills us. Got that? Ms. T wants a picnic meal, and she gave us the easiest thing on the menu—coleslaw. We don't even have to turn on the stove. Do you think we can put this homework assignment together and actually pass?"

"Sure. How hard can it be to cut up cabbage?" Alex said.

"Knowing you, you'll hack off a finger. Just sit down and let me do it," I said, reaching for the head of green cabbage I'd picked up at Ashton's after work. "Everyone else is doing something hard—cherry pie, spicy pulled pork, baked beans, homemade dinner buns."

"Coleslaw is good. We should be fine with that," Alex said.

I looked at him curiously. Alex was always so full of energy…it wasn't like him to be listless and agreeable. "What's up?" I said.

"Oh, nothing." Alex twiddled his fingers.

"Seriously," I said. "You are not acting normal."

"Well, I've been thinking. Your boss is looking for someone to blame for the tampering at Ashton's," Alex said.

"Yeah, I know," I said, remembering Scott's reaction to the garlic coffee.

"And there's something I haven't told you."

Now he really had my attention. "What?"

"I have a record," said Alex.

"So?" I said. "My grandparents have records too. Old ones. Barry Manilow, Elvis Presley. What's the big deal?"

"No, you idiot. A police record," Alex hissed.

"*What*!"

"It was no big deal, okay?" Alex glared at me. "A bunch of guys dared me to spray-paint stuff on the side of a building, and I got caught. I had no idea they set me up."

"What do you mean?"

"I mean the building was the police station. They knew it, I was the new kid trying to fit in, and I got hung out to dry.

But now I have a record for mischief and damage to public property and I don't know what else. If your boss finds that out, guess who is suspect number one?"

I didn't know what to say.

"Sometimes it sucks being the new kid," Alex said. He kept his eyes down. "We moved three times after we left here. I was pretty happy to come back this year."

"I think those records are kept confidential," I said.

"Sure," Alex said. "But the police have access to them. Trust me, if they're doing their jobs, they know."

I thought for a minute, and then I rummaged in the pockets of my jeans until I came up with a crumpled piece of paper. "You know, this might help," I said, showing it to Alex.

"An Ashton's job posting for a western regional manager?" Alex looked at me in disbelief. "How is that going to help?"

"No, on the other side." I showed him the name and number written on the back. "This is the old guy who came into the store with the garlic coffee. He seemed interested in helping with this tampering thing, and he sure wasn't afraid to stand up to Scott—"

"No!" Alex said. "I don't want anyone else knowing that I'm 'known to police.'"

"But—"

"No!" Alex was adamant.

I picked up a knife and began slicing the cabbage into fine shreds. "Graffiti isn't exactly a capital crime, you know."

Alex shrugged. "It was a stupid thing to do."

I continued slicing, but the knife hit a tough spot and I had to press down hard. The knife wouldn't move. I sawed at it, and finally the cabbage shredded. Alex pointed to some colored pieces among the green bits.

"What's that?" he said.

"I don't know." I stirred the pieces with a fingertip. "Looks like paper."

"We can't eat that. Where'd it come from?" Alex said.

I picked up the cabbage and examined it. Nothing looked out of the ordinary at first, but then I saw a fine line of white along the cut edge. I began peeling the leaves away. A coupon from Ashton's fell out.

"What? How did that get stuck in there?" I wondered, holding it up.

But Alex had paled. "It was no accident." He flipped it over so I could see the back, which he'd already caught a glimpse of. Scrawled in big black letters were the words *ASHTON'S SUCKS*.

I exhaled. "I have to call my boss."

"Trevor, you can't!" Alex panicked. "He'll think I did it."

"I have no choice." I pulled out my cell phone and found the Ashton's number on my contact list. Within seconds Scott was on the phone.

"Trevor, what's the matter? They had me paged in the middle of a phone conference."

"It's important. There's been another tampering incident." I explained about the note inside the cabbage. I heard Scott's sigh of despair over the phone.

"This is the end," Scott said. "There've been so many incidents now, I don't think there's any option. We'll have to close the store."

Chapter Nine

The bus pulled away from the curb on Friday afternoon with a belch of exhaust, leaving Robyn, Nick and I standing on the sidewalk.

"I just can't believe it," Robyn said. "You think Alex is the mystery food-tampering dude?"

"I didn't say that, exactly," I said.

"I hope he isn't. But I have reason to believe he might be."

"Why? Because he has a police record?" Nick asked.

I gaped at him. "How did you know that?"

"He told me right after he moved back. Kind of said it like he was bragging," Nick said.

"A police record for what?" Robyn wanted to know.

"Vandalism. To a police station," Nick said.

"*What*? Is he crazy?" Robyn said.

"Never mind that now," I said. "Scott said they have to close the store. We have to catch the culprit *now*, or everyone I work with is out of a job." I began walking in the direction of the shopping center a block away. The big Ashton's Fresh Marketplace sign was already visible. "That's why I want to try applying at this location. Maybe they'll let me transfer."

"It's awfully far away," said Robyn doubtfully. "How are you going to get to work?"

"It's only a bus ride from school, and hopefully my mom and dad won't mind picking me up," I said. "Besides, it's only until this mystery gets cleared up at the other Ashton's. When they open the store again, I'll go back."

"So the police don't think anything has been tampered with at this store?" Nick asked.

"I don't think they know that for sure, but everything seems to be showing up at the other store, and it's people in our area that have called in complaints," I answered. We started across the parking lot toward the Ashton's entrance. Robyn grabbed my arm and yanked me backward. I stumbled.

"Wait!" she said.

"What's the matter with you?" I said.

"Look over there." She pointed to man pushing a cart of groceries toward a new-looking sports car.

I looked. "So?"

"Look closer," she snapped. "It's Scott. Your boss."

"Hey, let's go say hi," I said.

"No!" said Robyn. "What's he doing here?"

"Um, maybe he's buying groceries like everyone else?" Nick offered. "He probably lives around here."

"Maybe," I said. "But he could buy groceries after work at our store. Why make a special trip?"

"Because he has a day off today and needed milk or something?" Nick shook his head. "You guys are making a big deal out of nothing."

"Let's get a little closer," Robyn suggested, ignoring Nick. We crept around some cars and knelt down beside an old truck, where we could get a clear view of Scott loading bags of food into the trunk of the sports car.

"Pretty fancy ride," Robyn whispered.

"Yeah," I said. I watched as Scott picked up an especially full bag and the bottom split open. A few bakery bags fell out, plus some plastic containers of berries, a bunch of cans, and boxes of juice, and what looked like pizzas from the deli.

"He's buying a lot of food for a single guy," said Robyn. "It seems odd."

"It's not odd at all," Nick pointed out. "He could be bringing dinner to a friend's house. He could be donating food to the food bank. He could be throwing a Stanley Cup party."

"Except that it's October," Robyn said sarcastically. "The Stanley Cup isn't until spring."

"Whatever. A party," Nick said. "There are a million reasons why Scott could be buying more food than he needs, reasons that have nothing to do with criminal activity. Besides, I can see your little pea-brain turning over new suspicions, but did you stop to think that Scott has every reason to want the tampering to stop? If the store closes, he loses his job, period. His livelihood is at stake. Do you really think he'd have anything to do with the tampering?"

"No," Robyn said reluctantly. "I guess it wouldn't make sense. I just don't know who it could be, and I don't want to suspect Alex."

"Trust me," Nick said with confidence. "There's a logical reason why Scott's here today. Maybe he's doing the same thing you are, Trev. Trying to apply for a job over here because he knows the other store is shutting down."

I shrugged. "Anything's possible." I glanced back over at Scott. "But not likely," I added under my breath.

Chapter Ten

"You guys want to come over?" I asked Robyn and Nick as the bus pulled up to our stop. We got off. "I have to work later, but…"

"No, come to my house," Robyn said. "I promised my aunt I'd babysit. You guys can help."

"Oh sure, Robyn. It's Friday, our short day at school, and you want me to spend the afternoon taking care of little kids," Nick said.

"They're cute. It'll be fun." Robyn led us down the block and pushed open her front door. "Hi!" she called.

"Robyn! Where were you? Did you forget Auntie Cheryl was coming with the kids?" Robyn's mom stepped out of the family room, dressed in a fancy shirt and jeans. "Hi, boys." She smiled at us.

"I didn't forget. We had an errand after school."

"You're supposed to let me know if you're not coming straight home," Robyn's mom said.

"My phone's dead." Robyn pulled her cell phone out of her pocket and laid it on the kitchen counter. Her mom frowned and plugged it in.

"Convenient," I muttered in Robyn's ear.

"Very," she whispered back. The doorbell rang, and a moment later a flood of noise and small fast-moving bodies burst through the door.

"Robynrobynrobyn!" Two little kids pelted down the short hall and threw themselves at Robyn. Nearly bowled over, she caught them, laughing.

"Hi, guys!" she said.

Robyn's aunt Cheryl put a baby down on the floor. He was round-faced and gurgling. He rolled onto his stomach and began to chew on the nearest thing he could grab—Nick's shoe.

"Ooh, yuck." Aunt Cheryl pulled it away from him, handed him a squishy plastic toy and passed the baby to me. "Could you hold him just for a second?" she said. She took off down the hall.

"Uh, sure," I said. The baby was a lot heavier than I expected, and he was wiggling. I clutched him tighter so I wouldn't drop him, and he let out a howl. "Shhhh!" I whispered, looking around hastily. Aunt Cheryl was in the kitchen talking to Robyn's mom, so I lugged the baby to the family room and put him carefully down on the carpet, where Robyn had set the other two up with toys. The mess was incredible— toy trucks and building blocks and dolls were strewn across the floor. The four-year-old was energetically smashing play dough into the rug. And they'd only been there five minutes!

"No, no, Grayden," Robyn said. "If you want to play with play dough, you have to be on the mat."

"Okay," said Grayden, continuing to squish the play dough into a bright pancake in the beige carpet.

"Here, let me help you," Robyn said, scraping the play dough up with her fingernails. A fair bit was still stuck to the carpet, but she got Grayden settled onto a foam mat. The little girl, Anna, sat with her lap full of toys and didn't move.

The baby drooled a puddle on a different section of carpet.

"Okay, kids, we're going," Robyn's mom said. "We'll just be a couple of hours."

"Thanks for babysitting, Robyn," Aunt Cheryl said gratefully. "You have no idea how much I've been looking forward to this. Grayden and Anna can have a snack soon. They didn't eat much at lunch. Robbie was fed just before I came, so he can have a bottle in about an hour or so. Okay? You guys have fun with Robyn and her friends," she said to the kids. She gave a little wave.

"Mommy, no go," Anna said, her bottom lip sticking out.

"Only for a little while. I'll be back soon," Aunt Cheryl said.

"No!" Anna's face went red, and she opened her mouth and began crying at the top of her lungs.

I expected her mother to change plans immediately on seeing this distress, but Aunt Cheryl gave us a bracing smile, grabbed her purse and headed for the door. The slam of it closing behind the women was an ominous signal that we were now responsible for these kids.

"Anna, it's okay." Robyn knelt down and gave the little girl a hug. "We're going to have fun!"

Anna wept.

"Mommy won't be gone long, and we can play games!" Robyn's voice was unnaturally bright.

Anna sniffled.

"Maybe we should have a snack first. You love smoothies. Want Robyn to make you a smoothie? With raspberries? Yum!" Robyn said.

Tears still streaming down her face, Anna nodded.

"Okay. Let's go. You can help!" Robyn said. She held out her hand. Anna took it, and they went to the kitchen together. I looked at the drooling baby and at Grayden, who was throwing balls of play dough at the wall.

"Hey, Nick, I'll help Robyn. You okay here with these two?" I didn't wait for an answer. I fled to the kitchen, where Robyn was pulling vanilla yogurt, raspberries and a jug of milk out of the fridge one at time with her free hand. Anna still clung to the other one. Robyn looked at me gratefully.

"Can you wash these raspberries and throw them in the blender? Please?" she said.

"Sure." I took the package from her, opened the lid and ran the whole thing under the tap. Robyn set up the blender and added ice, milk and yogurt. I dumped the berries in, not paying much attention, and she turned on the machine.

The contents whirled in the glass jug, making a weird grinding sound. Robyn stopped the blender and peered inside.

"That seems really loud," she said. "Maybe I put in too much ice." She recapped the blender and turned it back on. The sound continued. She stopped it and reached for a plastic cup. "I wonder if there's something wrong with our blender." She started to pour the smoothie into the cup.

I watched as the red liquid with black flecks flowed out of the glass container.

Wait a second, I thought. Black flecks? "Robyn, stop!" I said, as she handed the plastic cup to Anna.

"Why?" said Robyn.

"Because I think there's something wrong with that smoothie." I looked in the bottom of the glass container. Some black bits remained near the blade, floating in the remnants of smoothie. I picked one out. It felt spongy but solid, definitely not

part of a raspberry. "Let me see that cup."
I took the cup from Anna and stuck my
hand into it. She let out an outraged howl.

"Trevor! What are you doing?"
Robyn cried.

I fished through the goopy liquid,
searching with my fingertips for the
object I knew I would find. I held up a
chewed-up hunk of black rubber, drip-
ping with raspberry mush.

"Ew! What *is* that?" Robyn said.

"Hey, can I get some help out here?"
Nick hollered from the family room,
a note of desperation in his voice.

"Nick, come here. We have a situation," I called above Anna's howling
over the loss of her smoothie.

"Bring the baby," Robyn reminded
him, trying to shush Anna.

Nick came into the kitchen, lugging
Robbie as if he were holding a box of
dynamite. "What's up?"

I showed him the soggy lump of black rubber.

"Gross," he said. "What is it?"

"I think," I said. "It's what's left of a rubber spider." I emptied the cup into the sink. As the smoothie drained away, fragments of red fruit were left on the bottom of the sink, along with small bits of rubber. The remains of the spider, ground up by the blender. Robyn put her hand to her mouth.

"Oh my god," she whispered. "And I would have fed that smoothie to…" Her voice trailed off, and she swallowed hard, looking at Anna. "She could have choked."

"Yeah." I took a deep breath. "Someone tampered with those raspberries," I said grimly. "And now it's getting deadly."

Chapter Eleven

"I didn't do it!" Alex protested.

"Look, Alex, you have to be straight with us," I said. "The cops are going to question you. We already know you put a rubber spider in the grapes at Ashton's on my first day, and Scott suspects that. He's going to point suspicion at you."

"Especially since you have previous misdemeanors," Robyn said.

Alex stared at her, then at me.

"I never said a word," I told him.

"I did," Nick said. "You never made it a secret, man. You told me like you were proud of it."

Alex looked down. "Some kids think that's cool. Like you're tough, you know? I didn't know what you guys were like now. I mean, I knew you in kindergarten. That's a long time ago."

"Alex, you don't have to break the law to make friends," Robyn said.

"You don't get it, Robyn," Alex said wearily. "You've lived here your whole life, had the same friends since you were four. People expect you to prove something when you're new. You can't let them know you're scared when they test you."

"So spraying graffiti on a police station is a test?" asked Robyn.

"Basically, yeah. If you have the guts to do it, they respect you."

"Except they tricked you," said Robyn.

"I know," Alex said.

"Look," I said. "The fact is that Scott already suspects my friends because you were there the day that old lady freaked out with the spider. Alex has already said that if the police are doing their jobs, they'll know all about his record. So Alex is suspect number one."

"But I didn't do it," said Alex. "I wish you never told the police about the spider in the smoothie."

"We had to," Robyn said. "You can't withhold information from the police."

"Yeah, but now they think I did it," Alex said.

"We need to start investigating who else might be responsible, so you don't get framed," I said.

"Well, I know one person who has a pretty strong motive," Nick said.

"Who?" I asked.

"I doubt we're going to get a warm welcome here," Robyn said. She looked at the address, then the weed-ridden patch of front yard. "Are you sure this is the right place?"

I checked the scrap of paper in my hand. At Ashton's, I'd gotten the name of the woman who had been fired on my first day and found an old employee contact list in the staff room that still listed her address. "I think so." Nick and Alex had gone down the back alley to look for clues in the backyard and around the garbage bins.

Plastic toys littered the yard, and the front-window curtains blocked any view of the inside of the house. The screen door leaned sideways on one hinge.

A small flower bed contained nothing but dog droppings and a pile of old advertising leaflets.

I rang the bell. I waited a long moment, then a balding guy with a sleeveless T-shirt and three days' growth of beard opened the door. "Yeah?" he said roughly.

"Um. We're looking for Mattie Hoff. Is she here?" Robyn said.

The guy eyed us with suspicion. "What do you want with her?"

"I work at Ashton's. She…uh…gave me some advice before she left. I want to talk to her about it." I swallowed. This guy had a menacing quality about him, and I had no doubt that this was a very bad idea.

"Just a sec." The guy turned away. "Mattie! Someone here for you," he yelled.

Mattie appeared behind him, looking even worse, if it was possible, than the day I had seen her in the store. She wore ratty pajama pants and a grubby white hoodie with some kind of food stain on the front. Her hair was wild and unwashed, and the odor of cooking grease clung to her.

"What?" she said irritably.

I cleared my throat. "Hi," I said, feeling inadequate with both of them glaring at me.

"Hi." Mattie folded her arms across her chest.

Robyn nudged me in the ribs. We couldn't waste this chance.

"You probably don't remember me, but I was at Ashton's the day you left. You bumped into me on your way out and…said some stuff."

"Yeah?" Mattie rolled her eyes. "So what?"

This wasn't going well. Robyn gave me a desperate look. "The manager's a real jerk," I burst out. This was a lie, of course, but I figured it might get her to say something.

"Tell me something I don't know," Mattie snarled, but her expression had relaxed the tiniest bit.

"You said he'd do the same thing to me if I didn't watch out," I said, warming to this approach.

"Oh, yeah, kid. He'll treat you like crap. He does it to everybody."

"He's accused my friend of tampering with the food," I continued. "He never did, but someone's been messing with things there. It's been all over the news," I said, watching her expression carefully.

Her eyelids flickered. "I heard."

"And now," Robyn continued, "something awful has happened." She stopped and lowered her voice almost to a whisper. "Someone hid a rubber spider in a package of raspberries, and I ground it up in a smoothie and almost fed it to my little cousin. It could have killed her!"

Mattie did react then. "That's terrible," she said, recoiling. Her face grew red and her eyes narrowed. "Ashton's is garbage. I wouldn't work there again if they paid me a million bucks."

"What I want to know is why you kids are here, telling Mattie all this stuff," her husband said.

"Um." My mind went blank. "Well…because I'm getting treated the same way. And now my friend and I are suspects in the tampering, and I don't know what to do about it," I finished in a rush.

"Quit, dum-dum," said the guy.

"Uh, well, yeah," I said lamely.

"What I think," the guy leaned forward, menace etched in his face. "Is that you came here because you think Mattie might be messing around with that food."

"Oh. No. Not at all," I said, my knees shaking.

"It's Trevor's first job," Robyn put in quickly. "He doesn't want to quit. But we thought Mattie's experience with the company might help us understand what to do next. How they operate with their employees, you know."

The guy gazed at Robyn like she was speaking Swahili. "What?" he said.

"Look, Doug. They're just kids," said Mattie.

"Nosy kids," Doug said. "Better go, dude. Before I have to get mean."

Meaner than he already was? Yikes. I began to back down the steps. Doug pulled Mattie inside and slammed the door.

"Come on," I said. Robyn trailed me slowly down the porch.

"This stinks," she said.

"Yeah, it does." The wind had picked up, and the stench of the dog poop in the flower bed wafted around us. I held my nose.

"No, not that." Robyn looked at the flower bed and shook her head with impatience. "I mean, it stinks that we didn't get any information—" She broke off and her eyes widened. "Trevor, wait!"

"What are you doing?" I stared as Robyn ducked down beside the porch, right next to the piles of dung.

"Come here." She beckoned.

"Are you kidding?" I said in disbelief.

"Hurry!"

I knelt down beside her, almost gagging. "What?"

She pointed to the advertising flyers stacked beside the dog droppings.

"So?" I said.

"Look." Robyn grabbed the flyer on top. It was an Ashton's flyer. Several specials were circled. Dinner buns, bakery ginger cookies, coffee—and raspberries.

"She said she didn't shop there anymore. These are all items that were tampered with, Trevor," Robyn said in an excited whisper. "If she planned it, which items to do, we have the evidence right here!" She tucked the ad into her jacket. "Maybe there's more. Maybe there are items she circled that she hasn't tampered with yet, or groceries from the other incidents. We have to look!"

Fighting the overpowering smell, I helped her scrabble among the papers, looking for Ashton's ads. A small scraping noise made me look up. Above us was the living room window. The curtains were no longer drawn across it. A sick feeling of dread grew in my stomach. Doug stood there, glaring through the glass.

"Robyn, come on. We have to go!" I pulled her up.

"Wait, I found one!" She wrenched out of my grasp and reached for a leaflet.

"Now!" I hauled Robyn to her feet. I heard the sound of a gate latch clicking open and a series of booming, deep-throated barks. The creators of the poop were about to come around the corner of the house, and they didn't sound friendly.

"Run!" I yelled.

Chapter Twelve

Robyn squealed in panic as we raced down the street.

"Doug was watching you through the window. He saw you take the flyer," I said, my feet pounding on the concrete. The barking grew louder. I chanced a backward glance and saw two massive dogs streaking across the front lawns, their eyes fixed on us. "This way!"

I shoved Robyn between the nearest house and its neighbor.

"What are you doing? We're trapped!" Robyn shouted.

"We'll never outrun them. Jump the fence, quick!" I said.

Robyn leaped and got one leg over, but that was it. I shoved hard on her back and her other leg, and she toppled over the fence, landing with a crash. The dogs bounded into the space between the houses just as I vaulted myself upward. For a split second I hung half over the fence, the dogs snarling up at me, foamy drool flying in all directions as they scrabbled frantically at the wood. Then I fell backward to safety, into a pile of empty pop cans. The fence shuddered beside me as the dogs tried to rip it down, but I exhaled in relief.

"Come on," Robyn said urgently. "Let's get out of here before someone sees us."

"Or before Doug gets here." I waded out of the cans, and we ducked into the back alley and ran for it. I couldn't see Alex and Nick anywhere but hoped they'd had the good sense to get the heck out of there. We scooted down a side road, into a second back alley and through a few more backyards before we finally felt safe.

When we reached my front yard, we leaned against each other for support, puffing and gasping.

Robyn bent forward at the waist, gulping air. "I can't believe he set the dogs on us."

"He didn't like us snooping around. Which makes them look guilty." I collapsed on the grass.

Robyn straightened. "That's true. What if it's Doug? He has the same motive as Mattie. He's mad at the store for firing her." She pulled the flyer from her jacket, unfolded it and began to read.

"It's dated two weeks ago," she said. "So the timing is right if they planned to tamper with the foods that are circled." She looked at me. "We should go to the police with this."

I leaned over to examine the flyer. "But there are a lot of other things that are circled. Look." I pointed to the cheese, potato chips and frozen pizza that were circled on the second page. "This just looks like a shopping list. I don't know if the police would take this seriously. We could be using this as evidence to accuse someone who is innocent."

Robyn snorted. "Puh-leeze," she said. "Attacking us with their dogs is not the act of innocent people. Besides, those could be items that haven't been tampered with yet."

"My boss assumed Alex was guilty. Isn't this kind of the same thing?" I said.

"No offense, Trevor, but I think there's still a chance Alex is guilty," said Robyn.

"He has no motive."

"Does he need one? He loves practical jokes. Look at how he fools around in Foods class."

I had no answer to that. "I think we'd better go to Ashton's," I said.

"When in doubt, go to the scene of the crime?" Robyn said.

"Sort of. Scott should know about this. He can decide whether to call the police," I said, holding up the flyer. "Maybe this is nothing more than Mattie circling the specials before she got fired."

"And maybe wings will sprout from your nose and you can fly to Ashton's instead of walking. I don't think I can even move."

"Call Nick on your cell," I said. "They should be here by now." I could see Robyn's hands shaking—the aftereffects of nearly being torn into bite-size pieces. "Tell them to get out of there," I said.

Robyn pulled out her cell phone. "Nick?" she said into the phone. "Come to Trevor's house. Right now." She hung up and flopped down on the grass.

"Nothing like getting right to the point," I said, just as Nick and Alex rounded the corner.

"I'm stressed," Robyn replied. "I was just almost eaten. I have no time to be nice." She closed her eyes.

"What are you talking about?" Nick said.

"You explain," Robyn said to me. So I launched into the story of what had happened. By the time I finished, Nick's mouth was hanging open.

"And you made Alex and me look for clues in the garbage bins?" Nick said. "How come we got the boring job?"

"You're welcome to do mine," Robyn said, exhausted. She pulled herself to a sitting position. "I'm getting too old for this stuff. My hair will be gray by the time I'm sixteen."

Nick stared at Robyn. "Are you okay?"

"What do you mean? Don't I look okay?" said Robyn.

"You're the one who is always telling me and Trevor to get off our butts and do something," said Nick. "I'm the one who says we should just chill."

"I know. I'm unmotivated right now," said Robyn. "Those dogs terrified me. I need some junk food."

I waved the flyer at her. "If we go to Ashton's, we can get junk food. I'll buy."

"I'm not going near Ashton's," Alex said. "I'm out."

Robyn ignored him. "One of those giant chocolate bars with the caramel inside?"

"Sure," I told her.

"Okay. I'm there." Robyn stood up. "But just so you know, I'm not sharing."

"Hey! Give me my chocolate back," Robyn said in a furious whisper. "I said I wasn't sharing!"

Nick stuffed a piece in his mouth before handing back the bar. "It's physically impossible for a fourteen-year-old boy to be around chocolate without eating some. It's simple biology." He said.

Robyn snorted and broke off a piece, which she handed to me. "That's why I made Trevor buy the extra-large bar," she said. "I *knew* I'd have to share." We were waiting in line at customer service at Ashton's to see Scott. He was listening patiently to an elderly woman argue about the price of strawberries. She added her strawberries to the pile of returned merchandise on the counter, which included boxes of bakery cookies, several bags of buns, a can of cashews and a bunch of other stuff. When it was our turn, I moved up to the counter. "Trevor. What are you doing here." He didn't say it like a question, and he didn't look pleased to see us.

"I have something to show you," I said. I unrolled the flyer. "We paid a visit to Mattie, the lady you fired a few weeks ago. We found this outside her house."

Scott took the flyer and scanned it. "This is really good," he said, his expression thawing. "This could be real evidence. Some of these items were tampered with the week this flyer came out. Would you be willing to talk to the police about it?"

"Sure," I said.

"Thanks," Scott said. "This might be just what we need to finally put a stop to this whole nightmare." Scott ran a hand through his thinning hair, making it stand up in unruly spikes. "Head office didn't want to shut down the store, even temporarily, but with the police coming in, and the media...people just don't want to shop here. If we don't solve the case soon, the whole chain might be affected."

"That's terrible," Robyn said.

"Thanks for bringing this in, kids," Scott said. "I'll contact the police right away. Trevor, do you mind hanging around in case they want to talk to you?"

"No problem," I said. "I'm supposed to work in an hour anyway. I didn't bring my uniform though."

"I can bike back to your house to get it," Nick offered.

"Thanks, man," I said. Nick headed for the front door, where he had left his bike. Robyn and I watched while Scott paged Madison to come to the customer-service desk. Then he grabbed his cell phone and went into the little office behind the counter, giving me a quick thumbs-up.

"Should we wait here?" Robyn asked.

"I guess so." I leaned against the wall. As Madison took over the counter, the lineup grew longer. More and more people had returns, probably due to all the tampering scares. Madison motioned to me.

"Trevor, I know you're not on shift yet, but could you please deal with this stuff for me?" she pleaded, gesturing to the growing pile of returned items on the counter. "Just take the non-grocery and sealed items and put them back on the shelf. I checked those earlier and there's nothing wrong with them. Everything else has to be taken to the back and logged in the inventory list, then put in a bin for the police to check before we throw it away."

"I know," I said. "I've done it before." I took a cart and loaded it with stuff. "Come on, Robyn. Give me a hand." We walked through the store, replacing shampoo, toothpaste, a can of cashews, some sealed packages of bakery cookies, a box of microwave popcorn and a package of razors. There was a head of lettuce that was turning brown, an opened package of cheddar cheese and some strawberries left in the cart. "I have to go back to the stock area to type this stuff into the inventory list. Can you wait here?" I said.

"Sure," Robyn said.

I went through the double door that led to the loading dock and stock area. The inventory computer was old and junky and was located on a desk by the staff bulletin board. I logged on, then had to wait an eternity for the thing to boot up. While it whirred and clunked,

I glanced over the bulletin board. There were job postings, ads for the week's specials, updates on employee discounts, a thank-you card a staff member had sent in. A notice of congratulations to the new regional manager caught my eye. Something about it seemed familiar, but the guy who got the position was from a store in Vancouver. I didn't recognize the name at all.

The computer finally finished its start-up noises, and I typed in the new password—promotion. And that's when the idea hit. Promotion. I had seen a notice for the manager position before. Scott had given it to the old guy, and the old guy had written his phone number on the back of it. What if Scott had wanted that job? Blindly I typed in the items for disposal, then snatched the congratulation notice off the bulletin board and ran back out to where Robyn was waiting.

"Have a look at this!" I shoved the paper at her.

"What?" She scanned the notice and gave me a blank look. "So?"

I pulled her around the aisle display, where we were half-hidden from customers in the store. "Listen, what if there's someone else who has a reason to be angry? Someone who's angry with head office for being passed over for promotion again? This notice is dated three weeks ago. That's right when the tampering started!"

"Trevor, what are you saying?" Robyn asked.

"I'm saying if Scott wanted the promotion and didn't get it, he might be angry with the company. He might want to get back at them by making the store lose money or even shut its doors."

"And he's driving such an expensive car...maybe he was counting on the promotion this time to pay off debts,"

Robyn speculated. "We don't even know if he applied for the regional job though."

I rubbed my forehead. "I know. I wish there was some way to prove he wanted that job."

"Would he have applied over the computer? Or by mail?" Robyn asked.

"I have no idea," I said. "If the inventory computer is any example of Ashton's computer system, maybe he sent a paper package. That thing is practically an antique."

"Okay." Robyn gave me a devious smile. "Let's see if this works." She pulled out her cell phone and typed *Ashton's Fresh Marketplace head office* in the search bar. "It's a good thing I have a decent data plan," she said. The location information popped up, along with the phone number in Ontario. She tapped the link, and the phone dialed in. "I hope you'll help me pay for this call. My parents are going to hit the roof when they see it on the bill," she said. Before I could respond, a cool female voice answered.

"Ashton's Fresh Marketplace, Corporate Office. How can I help you?"

"Hi. I'm sorry to bother you, but I have a really important question. There's a possibility that some important papers might have been included by accident in an application that was sent to you by Scott O'Rourke from one of your Calgary stores. Is there any way you could check for me to see if there was extra stuff with that package?"

"Listen, how old are you?" The female voice sounded annoyed.

"I'm fourteen. I know this is a huge bother, but it's really important," Robyn pleaded.

"Do you work for Ashton's?"

"No, but my friend Trevor does," Robyn said. "Please? We have a huge mix-up here, and I don't know of any other way to check."

"I'm sorry." The voice softened a bit. "But I can't. I do have Scott's application here, but he would have to call himself to get any information about it."

"All right. I'll ask him," Robyn said. "Thank you." She hung up and gave me a triumphant grin. "We got him!" she whispered.

"You're really smart," I said in admiration.

"And I didn't even have to bend the truth that much," Robyn said. "Now, the question is, how would someone go about tampering with the food?"

"The security cameras are on even after hours, so it's not like he could do it after the store closes," I said. "If it was me, I'd tamper with it somewhere else."

Robyn grabbed my wrist. "Trevor! You're a genius!"

"I am?" I said.

She gave my arm a little shake. "Somewhere else! Don't you get it?"

The light dawned. "You mean the other Ashton's store."

"What if he's buying stuff at the other store, altering it at home, then bringing it here?" Robyn said.

"The security cameras would still see him putting stuff on the shelves," I said.

"He's the store manager though. Wouldn't that just look like he was working?" said Robyn.

"Maybe...but usually guys like me do that. I think it would look weird after a while if you backtracked the videos and saw Scott always putting items away on the shelves, especially ones that were tampered with," I said. I thought for a minute. The biggest piece of the puzzle was still a mystery. And then, in a flash of inspiration, I knew. "Wait a second," I told Robyn. "Guys like me!

I've been part of this whole tampering thing all along!"

"What?" she said.

"Guys like me. We shelve the packaged returns from customer service."

"That doesn't explain the raspberries. You don't put those back if they're returned."

"Sometimes people change their minds at the cash register. I take back fruit all the time because someone decided it was too expensive or something. In fact, I even remember putting raspberries back, along with some strawberries and grapes," I said.

"And the peppered cookies?" Robyn said.

"That's only happened once, probably because Scott would have had to tamper with them right in the bakery. It was too risky to keep doing it. Same with the bulk bins. The other peppered bakery goods were bagged buns and bagels.

He could have done that at home," I speculated. Another thought blindsided me. "Robyn, we probably just did it again! What did we just put out on the shelves?"

"Um, razors. Shampoo. Microwave popcorn," she said.

"I don't think anything would be wrong with that stuff," I said.

"There were some cashews," Robyn suggested. "And toothpaste and... cookies. Sealed packages though."

"We'd better check," I said grimly. I found the cashews, but the tin looked completely sealed. We went back to the bakery and found the cookies, but they also looked well sealed. I was about to put them back when Robyn stopped me.

"Wait a minute. Look at the labels," she said. "They're all wrinkled."

I picked at one with my thumbnail, and the edges lifted up fairly easily. "But the package itself doesn't look opened," I said.

"Think outside the cookie box, Trevor," she said. "Do those look like oatmeal cookies to you?"

"No," I said slowly. "They look more like peanut butter."

"That's what I thought. But the label says oatmeal. What's on the other package?"

I checked. "This one says peanut butter."

"That's no accident," Robyn said. "I'll bet anything that someone switched these labels on purpose."

"That's not really tampering, is it?" I said.

"Of course it is," Robyn said. "What if someone had an allergy? Peanut allergies are really serious. If someone with an allergy thought these were oatmeal cookies when they're really peanut butter, they could go into anaphylactic shock. They could die!"

A sick feeling grew in my stomach. Just as I was about to tell Robyn we needed to go to the police ourselves, I felt someone grasp my shoulder, hard. I turned to see who, and shock jolted through my body.

Chapter Thirteen

"Trevor." Scott leaned close. My knees buckled. "I need to talk to you."

I swallowed. "About what?"

"The police detective is on her way. You said you'd speak with her about the flyer you found at Mattie's house."

"Oh. Yeah. Right." I breathed a silent sigh of relief.

"Come on up to my office." He steered me toward the back of the store. Robyn watched me with scared wide eyes. Scott propelled me up the stairs, past the staff room and into his small corner office. He locked the door. "Have a seat."

My heart thudded, and my hand closed around my cell phone in my pocket. I sat down on the edge of the chair opposite the desk. Scott sat behind his desk and leaned back, relaxed. "Where's the detective?" I said.

Scott gave a light chuckle. "I think you know the answer to that."

"No." I tried to keep my voice steady.

"He's sitting right here, in front of me. Think of yourself as quite the investigator, don't you, Trevor?"

"Not really," I said blandly.

"Oh, I think you do. And we need to have a little chat about how nosy people should mind their own business." The menace in his words was unmistakable. I fumbled discreetly for my phone. I hoped I was hitting 9-1-1, but it was impossible to know without seeing. I did not like the look on Scott's face at all, and the locked door made me feel like a prisoner. "I thought you wanted me to talk to the police."

"I did, until I received a phone call from head office a few minutes ago. They had some questions regarding why a young girl was asking questions about my application."

I gulped.

"And then I overheard you and your friend today. I would have interrupted, but it sounded very interesting."

I felt my stomach slide down to my knees. "You heard…?"

"Everything," Scott said. "What's so amazingly stupid of your little gang of amateur detectives is that no one thought about how incriminating it would look to have you, who started working here right after the tampering began, place tampered items on the shelves. You have Madison as a witness that you were the last known person to handle those packages of cookies. One of you could easily have switched the labels. You're kids. Do you think anyone is going to believe your gang of idiots over the word of the store manager, who has everything to lose with bad publicity for the store?"

My temper flared. "Everything to lose—except that's exactly what you want, isn't it? Ever since you lost the promotion for regional manager. That's why you've been messing around with all the products, to make the company go out of business. You're a sore loser. No wonder they didn't promote you!"

"Listen, you little butt-wipe, you know nothing about why I did anything."

"You could have killed somebody. A little girl almost drank a smoothie filled with rubber spider bits! Someone with a peanut allergy could have bought those cookies that you switched the labels on! What kind of sick person puts a job ahead of a human life?"

"I never planned to hurt anyone," Scott said between gritted teeth. "Your buddy Alex gave me the idea after that old girl had a fit over the spider in the grapes. I wanted head office to get a taste of what the bad times feel like. I've worked my tail off for this store, and this is how they repay me? By passing me over again? This was the fourth time I tried to go higher up."

"So it *was* you," I accused.

"Yeah, it was. So what? No one got hurt."

"You almost killed a little kid," I yelled. "You idiot. What were you thinking?"

"Rubber spiders are pretty easy to see," he shot back. "No one was supposed to eat them."

"Well, they almost did," I said flatly. "And now that I know about it, you're toast." I cast a brief glance at the locked door.

Scott caught the direction of my glance. "Well, no. Actually, I'm not. Because I've put in a call to Officer Anderson to let her know that you and your friend Alex confessed to being responsible for the tampering."

"You can't do that." My mouth dried out.

Scott answered me with a wolfish grin. "Just watch me. You're pretty young for jail, but maybe you'll get lucky and get sentenced to community service."

I gaped at him.

"And if you start yapping about our little talk up here...well, it'll be obvious that you're just a teenager looking to get out of trouble. Happens all the time. And so do accidents, by the way. Especially in stores like this, where there's heavy equipment in the back, if you get my meaning."

I did. And I didn't like it one bit. Fury overwhelmed me. I stood up so fast, the chair tipped backward and clattered to the floor. Before I could react further, Scott leaped over the desk and shoved me. I stumbled over the chair, and as Scott advanced, I rolled away, kicking the chair toward him. He pushed it aside, never taking his eyes off me. I scrambled to my feet, and we circled the small office like fighters in the ring. He rushed at me. My reflexes kicked in, and I got in one solid punch. Blood spurted from his nose. He reeled a bit, but anger lit his eyes and he pressed forward, backing me into a corner. I was trapped.

I swung my fist again, but this time Scott blocked my arm. He drove me into the desk, grabbed my throat and squeezed. "Bad move, Trevor," he said. I struggled, but his grip was like iron. "Maybe you'll be a little more cooperative now."

"Not likely," I gasped. He was leaning over me, his stomach unprotected. I drove my fist hard into his belly. It was like hitting a pillow. He loosened his grip as the breath flew out of him. I kicked, landing a hard blow to his knee, and shoved him away. As he fell to the floor, I made a break for the door.

Scott's hand shot out in a flash of speed I hadn't expected. He grabbed my ankle and I tripped, crashing to the floor. A solid weight landed on my back, and suddenly Scott was so close, I could smell the stench of sweat and his foul, coffee breath.

"Brushing your teeth would be good,"
I grunted.

In answer, Scott leaned on me
harder, driving my face into the floor.
"Listen, Trevor, and listen good. You're
going to get up and forget we ever had
this conversation. You breathe one word
to the police, and I swear they'll find
you hanging by your feet in the meat
locker with your insides hanging out.
You get me?"

I gulped.

Scott pressed my face a little harder
into the floor to make his point. "I'm not
going to jail because some snot-nosed
kid is playing detective."

"Oh yes you are!" I heard Robyn
shout from the hall. A sharp thud at
the door made us both jump. Before
we could react, a second thud sent the
door flying open, cracking the door-
frame. A police officer stood there, her
gun drawn. "Police! Move away from

the kid!" she shouted, aiming at Scott. "With your hands out where I can see them. Get flat on the ground. Now!"

Stunned, Scott obeyed. With the gun trained on him, the officer unclipped handcuffs from her gun belt. "Put your hands behind your back and then don't move," she warned him. She snapped the cuffs on his wrists.

Robyn and Nick rushed in. Robyn dropped down beside me. "Trevor," she said, grabbing me in a suffocating hug. "We thought he was going to kill you!"

I wriggled out of Robyn's grasp. "Me too." My whole body shook and twitched from the rush of Adrenalin. I took a deep breath, looking with loathing at Scott's prone body on the floor.

"I hope it was worth it," I said to him. I turned to my friends. "Come on. Let's go.

Chapter Fourteen

The story broke in the news the next
day. My parents, as usual, were furious
that we had been solving another
mystery they knew nothing about. They
grounded me when they found out I'd
been held hostage by my store manager.

"Why do you have to keep getting
into these situations?" my mother raged.

"Why can't you just play video games like every other kid?"

I was let out for a short reprieve when Nick, Robyn and Alex showed up at the door. "Don't let him leave the yard," Mom warned my friends, "or I'm tying him up on a leash."

"No problem," Alex said. "We'll keep an eye on him."

We sat down under a tree on the grass, and I felt the tension I'd carried for days finally ease. "So, thanks for coming to my rescue, Robyn. But how come they arrested Scott right away? He said that he was going to deny everything and blame it on me. Why didn't they question him first?"

"Because we heard everything," Robyn said. "I guessed from the look on Scott's face that he had clued in to what we suspected. I went back to customer service. I was going to tell Madison everything and call the police. Then the police detective showed up. Scott had actually called her like he said he would—his bad luck."

"Okay," I said. "But that still doesn't explain why the police didn't give Scott a chance to weasel out of everything. Police don't usually bust down doors unless they have a reason."

"We did," Nick said.

"You called me," said Robyn. "On your cell phone."

"No, I didn't," I said.

"Yes, you did," Robyn insisted. "My phone rang when I was back at customer service."

I thought back to before the fight, when I knew things were starting to look bad. "I tried to call nine-one-one," I recalled.

"You must have hit the buttons for your contact list and got me," Robyn said. "Because I picked up and could hear everything that was going on between you and Scott."

"And then," Nick said proudly, "she had the most evil idea ever."

"Remember when Scott paged Madison to come and help at customer service when we were standing there?" Robyn said. "I watched him do it. So I clicked on the paging system and held the phone to it. The whole store heard his confession, heard him threatening you, the works."

"So there was no way he could deny anything, not with fifty million witnesses," said Alex.

"And when the fight started, the police officer radioed for backup and went up there right away. She told us to stay downstairs, but there was no holding Robyn back, so we followed her," Nick added.

"It seemed like that fight lasted for hours," I said.

"It was seconds," Robyn said. "Once we knew Scott wasn't fooling around, we were there right away."

"Well," I said, relieved, "Scott will end up in jail for sure, and the food tampering is over. It sounds like everything's wrapped up."

"Almost," said Alex.

"What do you mean?" I said.

"Um, Ms. T is failing us in Foods unless we do a makeup project."

I clutched my hair with both hands. "Oh, no! Not another cooking project… I can't handle the stress."

"Honestly, Trevor," Robyn said. "You just took down a serious criminal—one who threatened to kill you. Foods class isn't that bad."

"Oh, yeah?" I said. "You've never worked with Alex!"

Michele Martin Bossley is the author of twenty novels for young people, including six Orca Currents mysteries featuring Robyn, Nick and Trevor. A frequent speaker at writing conferences and schools, Michele divides her time between writing and parenting her four sons. She lives in Calgary, Alberta.